Rude RUBY

ORCHARD BOOKS
Carmelite House, 50 Victoria Embankment, London EC4Y 0DZ
Orchard Books Australia
Level 17/207 Kent Street, Sydney, NSW 2000

First published in 1998 under the title
RUBY THE RUDEST GIRL by Orchard Books
This updated version published in 2015

ISBN: 978 1 40833 639 7

A CIP catalogue record for this book is available
from the British Library.

1 3 5 7 9 10 8 6 4 2

Printed and bound by CPI Group (UK) Ltd, Croydon, CR0 4YY

The paper and board used in this book are made from wood
from responsible sources.

Orchard Books is an imprint of Hachette Children's Group and published by
the Watts Publishing Group Limited, an Hachette UK company.

www.hachette.co.uk

Rude
RUBY

Laurence Anholt

Illustrated by Tony Ross

ORCHARD

www.anholt.co.uk

Hee, hee, hello everyone!
My name is **Ruby** and I have the
funniest family in the world.
In these books, I will introduce you
to my **freaky family**.

You will meet people like…

Tiny Tina

Mucky Micky

Poetic Polly

Brainy Boris

Bendy Ben

Brave Bruno

Hairy Harold

But this book is all about…ME! It's
called **Rude Ruby**.

When I was a little girl, I was **awfully** rude. People called me Ruby, the rudest girl in the **galaxy**.

PRRRRRRP !

My favourite words were **rude** words. My favourite noises were **rude** noises.

My favourite games were…guess what? **RUDE GAMES**!

Everything I said was rude.
Everything I did was rude.

People said, "Ruby is only a small girl, how can she be so rude?"

I am sure you are not a rude person. If a nice boy asked you to play, I expect you would say, "Yes, please. Thank you for inviting me." But what I said was...

Then I laughed. "Tee, hee!"

If a kind old lady helped you across the road, I'm sure you would say, "Thank you. It is kind of you to help me." But what I said was... "You are a crumbly old warthog, with a nose like a prune."

Then I laughed even more.
"Tee, hee, hee!"

I don't know why I was so rude.
My mum is not rude. My dad is
not rude. My brother and sister are
always polite.

PRRRRPPPO

But I pulled **horrid** faces. And I made **rude** sounds.

And I did **disgusting** things with my food.

My brother and sister said, "Ruby, you are so rude, you belong in a cage in a zoo."

And I said, "You are like two big baboons. It is you who should be in a zoo."

I made them both cry. And I just
laughed again.
"Tee, hee, hee, hee!"

My kind mummy said, "Ruby, your brother and sister are right. You are so rude you belong in a cage in a zoo."

And I said, "You have a nose like an elephant and ears like a bat. It is **you** who should be in a zoo."

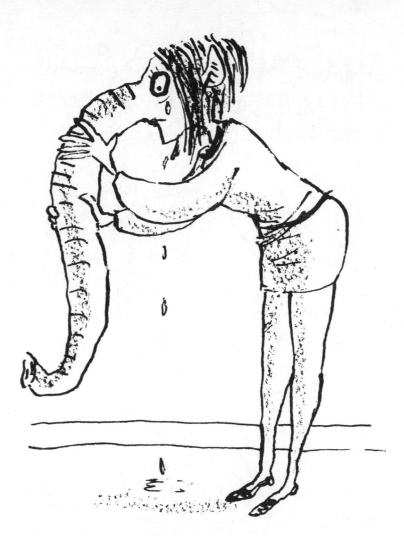

Then my mother cried too. And I laughed more than ever. "Tee, hee, hee, hee, hee!"

My lovely daddy said, "Ruby, your brother and sister and mother are right. You are too **rude** to live in a nice house, with a nice family. You belong in a cage in a zoo."

And I said, "You look like a camel and smell like a skunk. It is **you** who belongs in a zoo."

My dad said, "You have gone **too far**, Ruby. Here comes the van to take you to the zoo."

The sign on my cage said, "COME AND SEE RUBY, THE RUDEST GIRL IN THE GALAXY."

COME AND SEE
RUBY
THE RUDEST GIRL
IN THE GALAXY

Everyone gathered around.
Everyone came to see **the
rudest girl**.

I was not happy in my cage.
I knew I had gone too far.

I was **sorry** about the rude things
I had said.

I looked at the nice animals in the zoo. They were not rude at all. They were all well behaved.

I thought for a **long** time.
I decided to be polite.

When the people came to look at me, I said, "Good afternoon. My name is Ruby. How do you do?"

The people were cross. They had come to see **Ruby, the rudest girl**. But I was not rude at all. I was a **polite** little girl.

The people went away.

I called out, "Thank you for coming to see me. Please come again another day."

The zoo keeper unlocked my cage. "You are too polite to be here. You belong in a **nice** house, with your **nice** family. You belong at home."

So I went back to my nice, polite family. They were **very** pleased to see me. "Welcome home, Ruby, now that you are a polite girl."

That is why I stopped being
Ruby, the rudest girl.

That is how I turned into **Ruby, the politest girl in the galaxy**.

Everything I said was polite.
Everything I did was good.

"Quiet now. Listen! Ruby is going to say something. Listen, everyone. The politest girl has something to say…"

"What is it, Ruby? What polite thing would you like to tell us? Ruby is going to speak." I stood up **nice and straight**. I smiled at everyone politely. Then I said...

Hm...
Hm...

"OH, RUBY! That is definitely NOT polite at all!"

And I said, "TEE, HEE, HEE, HEE, HEE!"

THE END

MY FREAKY FAMILY

COLLECT THEM ALL!

RUDE RUBY   978 1 40833 639 7

MUCKY MICKY   978 1 40833 764 6

POETIC POLLY   978 1 40833 754 7

BRAINY BORIS   978 1 40833 756 1

BRAVE BRUNO   978 1 40833 762 2

TIINY TINA   978 1 40833 760 8

BENDY BEN   978 1 40833 758 5

HAIRY HAROLD   978 1 40833 752 3

Also available as an ebook